this book is DEDICATED to
little baby Venema
and maybe it can help her
just a tiny bit
to feel at home in this
noisy, CRAZY, messy, mazy
WORLD

NiGHT WiNDOWS

aart-Jan Venema

My parents said, "Give the city a chance.
At second glance you'll find that the heat
And the beat of the streets
Will have you up on your feet.
Wait and see."

But all *I* could see was endless grey, day after day,
With no-one to talk to and no-one to play.
It didn't seem much fun to me.

I went downstairs to find a haze of rage,
Angry faces filling the space,
Shoving, rushing, crushing, where to? Who knew.
I needed to get out of this place!

I stepped outside for some air,
Thinking, "This isn't fair, I don't care
What they say. No way,
I'll pack my bags and run away."
But then I looked up at the block and I saw
Some things I hadn't seen before.

A writer, a cook, five kids
And – look! Three cats, a nest
A sparkling chest, a girl who sews,
A garden that grows, a bat and two crows.
It was like watching a show.

The next night, I went back outside.
I felt kind of bad as I spied, wide eyed,
But it seemed to be the only
Way to feel less lonely.

This time I saw a bird with a twig, a man in a wig,
A garden gnome, two statues of stone,
A ball being thrown,
A lady singing, two lamps swinging,
A ghost haunting the building.

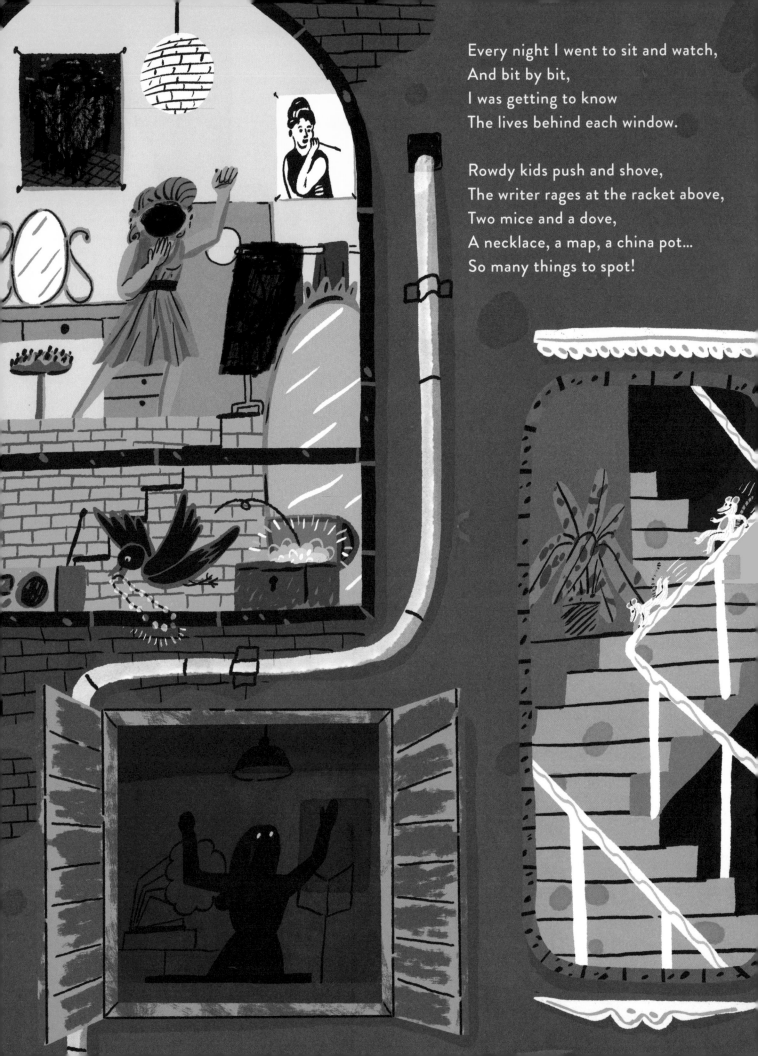

Every night I went to sit and watch,
And bit by bit,
I was getting to know
The lives behind each window.

Rowdy kids push and shove,
The writer rages at the racket above,
Two mice and a dove,
A necklace, a map, a china pot...
So many things to spot!

I had company the next night –
The writer who had struggled to write!
He said, "I've lost sight
Of what's real and what's not,
I'm losing the plot.

"But from here, things seem clearer.
Can you see a cat and six hats?"
"Seven," I said, "there's one on your head!
And two ties – one blue, one red."

He nodded, "It's time to rearrange,
Make some changes,
Introduce a few strangers.
What do you think?"
He gave me a wink.

The writer got straight to it,
Fixing up, mixing up,
And suddenly,
Things were changing rapidly,
Neighbours talking happily,
Finding new realities.

And then to my surprise,
There were other kids outside,
Laughing, playing, racing, chasing,
Listening to what each other was saying.
It was amazing!

My new friends and I cooked up a plan
To continue what we'd started,
We'd have a party!

With a hearty meal,
Music and dancing,
Take the chance to dress up fancy,
Spend time together,
Get to know each other better.

As a team,
We cooked and cleaned;
Peeling carrots,
Steaming greens.
Slicing, chopping,
Rinsing, mopping,
Never stopping, swapping stories,
Like we'd known each other for years.

I escaped the kitchen heat
And sat for a while in my familiar seat.
I spotted a cup of tea, a tail that wags,
A wheelbarrow, a globe, two shopping bags,
A sleepy cat, a string of flags.

Everyone mending and lending,
Preparing and sharing,
Trying on daring outfits for wearing.

At last it was the big night.
Everything was just right.
To my delight,
It had all gone to plan!

We danced and played
And laughed and sang.
Eating and drinking,
Spinning and grinning,
Chatting, relaxing,
It felt like the beginning
Of something special indeed.

These days there's so much to see and do,
Friends old and new...
I'm too occupied to sit on my own outside.
But sometimes at twilight
I catch sight of the light
Of the lives behind the windows,
And I know that I've made it my own.

This busy, dizzying,
Noisy, crazy, messy, mazy,
Living, breathing,
Heart beating,
Never sleeping,
Or stopping,
Whopping great
City I call home.

NIGHT WINDOWS
Published by Cicada Books Limited
Illustrated by Aart-Jan Venema
Written by Ziggy Hanaor

British Library Cataloguing-in-Publication Data.
A CIP record for this book is available from the
British Library. ISBN: 978-1-908714-56-5

First published: UK, 2018; USA, 2019
© Cicada Books Limited, all rights reserved.

Aart-Jan Venema is an illustrator living and
working in The Hague, Netherlands. He takes
inspiration from science fiction and history,
and from the little adventures that he finds in
everyday life. His illustrations have featured in
the *Guardian, New Yorker, Wall Street Journal*,
Green Man Festival and many others.

Cicada Books Limited
48 Burghley Road
London NW5 1UE
www.cicadabooks.co.uk